Letters from Lila

by Hinda Malachi
illustrated by Marsha Slomowitz

**Harcourt**

Orlando   Boston   Dallas   Chicago   San Diego

Visit *The Learning Site!*

www.harcourtschool.com

Dear Grandma,

    Thank you for taking me out to eat. It was so much fun! Mexico City is an amazing place.

Love,
Lila

Dear Grandma,

   We will be moving soon to a city called Walnut Creek. It is in the United States.

   I asked if I could live here with you and stay at my school. Dad said no.

Love,

Lila

Dear Grandma,

    We took a plane from Mexico City to San Francisco. Then we took a train to Walnut Creek. It raced along like the Metro. It was fun, but I miss home.

                        Love,

                        Lila

Dear Grandma,

One thing I like about Walnut Creek is the clear sky. We don't have as much smog here as Mexico City does.

Today I am starting at my new school.

Love,
Lila

Dear Grandma,
    My new teacher is Ms. Frank. She
gathered the children to meet me.
I met a girl named Kate. I don't
know if she likes me. I miss you.
                                    Love,
                                    Lila

Dear Grandma,
   I keep your letters with me. They
are in my backpack now! No one else
is eating lunch with me yet. Many kids
are clustered at the next table.
   I miss you.

                          Love,
                          Lila

Dear Grandma,
    The class I like best so far is music.
I have begun to play the recorder.
    Mom wants me to invite a classmate
over after school. I might ask Kate.
                              Love,
                              Lila

Dear Grandma,

In gym, we play a game called T-ball. It's like baseball. I'm very good! Twice I raced to first base. Kate is on my team.

Love,

Lila

Dear Grandma,

Dad says he will take me to San Francisco soon. I gathered my nerve and asked Kate if she would like to come. She said yes!

Love,
Lila

Dear Grandma,

Kate says thank you for the drawing. She has never been to Mexico City.

We had fun in San Francisco. We wandered all over with Dad.

Love,
Lila

Dear Grandma,

At school we are going to have a party for Cinco de Mayo.

Ms. Frank asked me what I used to do on this day. All of a sudden I wanted to be back home.

Love,
Lila

Dear Grandma,

   Our Cinco de Mayo party was fun.
Ms. Frank asked me if the classroom
looked like home. I told her it looked great,
but now I wonder which place is home.

Love,
Lila

Dear Grandma,

   Ever since our Cinco de Mayo party, my classmates have more to say to me.

   In two weeks, I will have finished second grade! I have made a few friends.

Love,
Lila

Dear Grandma,
    Mom tells me I can visit you this summer! I have some plans here, too. In July I'll go to summer camp with Kate. We'll swim and play soccer.

Love,
Lila

Dear Grandma,

    I can hardly wait to see you! I'll put some photos in this letter. They show us on the trips we took around Mexico City. Maybe we can visit some of these places again.

Love,

Lila